lauren child

I will not ever NEVER eat a tomato

featuring Charlie and Lola

ORCHARD BOOKS

This book is for Soren

who is crazy about tomatoes

but would never eat a baked bean

with love from Lauren

who is keen on Marmite

but would rather not eat a raisin

www.hachette.co.uk

This edition published in 2010

ORCHARD BOOKS 338 Euston Road, London NW1 3BH

First published in 2000

Orchard Books Australia Level 17/207 Kent Street, Sydney, NSW 2000

Text & Illustrations © Lauren Child 2000 & 2010

First published in hardback in 2000

Printed in China

The right of Lauren Child to be identified as the author and illustrator of this book

A CIP catalogue record for this book is available from the British Library.

Orchard Books is a division of Hachette Children's Books,

an Hachette UK company.

ISBN 978 184616 886 4

3 5 7 9 10 8 6 4 2

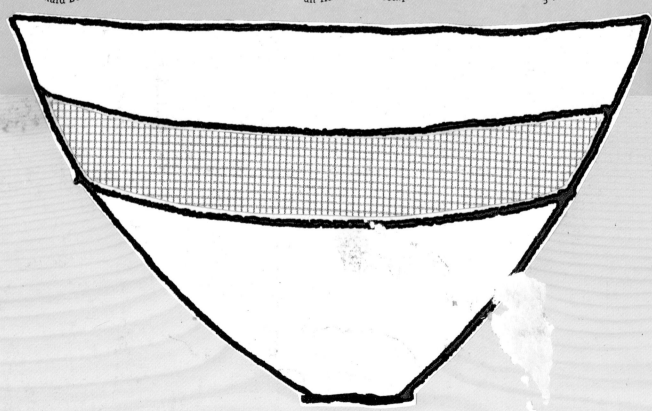

I have this little sister Lola.
    She is small and very funny.
    Sometimes I have to keep an eye on her.
Sometimes Mum and Dad ask me to give her her dinner.
    This is a hard job because she is a very fussy eater.

Lola won't eat carrots, of course.
She says carrots are for rabbits.

I say, "What about peas?"

Lola says,
"Peas are too small
and too green."
One day I played a good trick on her.

She was sitting at the table
waiting for her dinner.
And Lola said,
"I do not eat

Peas   or   carrots   or   potatoes

or   Mushrooms   or   spaghetti

or   eggs

or

sausages.

I do not eat

cauliflower   or   cabbage   or

baked beans

or   bananas      or   oranges.

And I am not keen on

apples   or   rice      or   cheese

or

fish fingers.

And
I absolutely
will not ever
never
eat a tomato."   (My sister hates tomatoes.)

And I said,
          "That is lucky

because we are not having any of those things.

We are not going to eat any peas or carrots
or potatoes or mushrooms or spaghetti or eggs or sausages.

There will be no cauliflower or
cabbage or baked beans or bananas or oranges.

We don't have any apples or rice or cheese or fish fingers

and **certainly** no tomatoes."

Lola looks at the table.

"But why are those Carrots there, Charlie?

And I said,
"Oh you think these are carrots.
These are not carrots.
These are orange twiglets from Jupiter."

"They look just like carrots to me," says Lola.
"But how can they be carrots?" I say.
"Carrots don't grow on Jupiter."

"That's true," says Lola.
"Well I might just try one
if they're all the way from Jupiter.
Mmm, not bad," she says, taking another bite.

Then Lola sees some peas.

"I don't eat peas,"

says Lola.

I say,

"These are not peas,

of course they are not,

these are green drops

from Greenland.

They are made

out of green

and fall from the sky."

"But I don't eat green

things," Lola says.

"Oh goody,"

I say.

"I'll have

your share;

green drops

are so

incredibly

rare."

"Well

maybe

I'll nibble

just one

or two.

Oh," says

Lola, "quite

tasty."

Next Lola spies the potato.
"I will not eat potato
so don't even try,
       not even mash."

"Oh,
this
isn't mash.
People often
think that but no,
this is cloud fluff from
the pointiest peak of Mount Fuji."
"Oh well, in that case a large helping for me;
I love to eat cloud."

"Charlie,"
she says,
"they look like fish fingers to me,
and I would
never
eat a fish finger."

"I know that, but these are not fish fingers. These are ocean nibbles from the supermarket under the sea - mermaids eat them all the time."

"Oh, I've been to that supermarket,
one time with Mum.
Yes, I know the ones.
I think I've had them before," Lola says, gobbling.
"Are there any more?"

And then Lola says,

"Charlie will you pass me one of those?"

And I say,

"What, one of those?"

"Yes, Charlie,
one of those."
And I can't believe my eyes
because guess what she is pointing at,
the tomatoes.

And I say,

"Are you sure?

Really?

One

of these?"

And she says,

"Yes, of course, moonsquirters are my favourites.

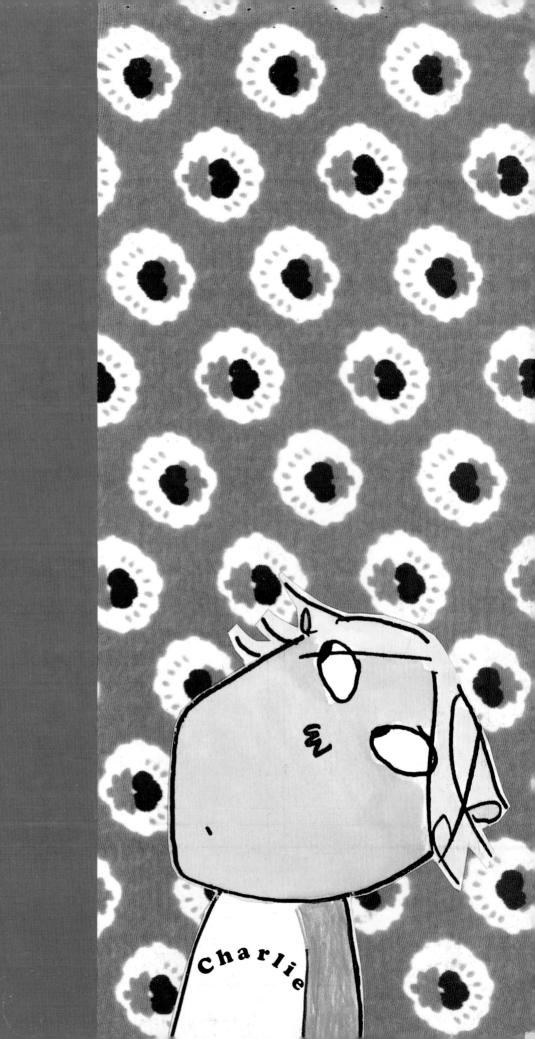

"You didn't think they were toMatoes, did you, Charlie?"